THE SMURFS

A Smurfin' Big Adventure!

by Fern Alexander
illustrated by Mel Milton

Simon Spotlight
New York London Toronto Sydney

SIMON SPOTLIGHT

An imprint of Simon & Schuster Children's Publishing Division 1230 Avenue of the Americas, New York, New York 10020

For information about special discounts for bulk purchases, please contact Simon & Schuster Special Sales at 1-866-506-1949 or business@simonandschuster.com.
Manufactured in the United States of America 0611 LAK   10 9 8 7 6 5 4 3 2
ISBN 978-1-4424-2274-2

It was the night of the Blue Moon Festival, and everyone was excited! Suddenly, Smurfette heard panicked screams. Gargamel, the evil wizard, was near! Clumsy screamed and ran into the forest. Smurfette, Grouchy, Brainy, Gutsy, and Papa ran after him. Just then the blue moon appeared in the sky and Clumsy fell through a mysterious portal. Quickly they jumped in after him—and ended up in a world they had never seen before.

"Where the smurf are we?" Grouchy asked.

"We are up Smurf Creek without a paddle," Gutsy said, pointing to the portal. It was beginning to close!

Just then Azrael, the cat, came flying through the portal. The Smurfs scattered. If Azrael was around, Gargamel wasn't far behind! Azrael pounced on Smurfette, but only caught a mouthful of her hair. Next he scampered off to catch Clumsy. Clumsy jumped into an open box, which was soon carried off by a man getting into a taxi. They had to get Clumsy back!

As the Smurfs left the portal behind, Papa tried to reassure them. "When the blue moon rises here, the portal will open again," he said.

Meanwhile, Gargamel also arrived through the portal. He was delighted when Azrael showed him the ball of Smurfette's hair! His wish to be the strongest wizard of all might finally come true. All he needed was a lab where he could squeeze enough Smurf essence out of her hair to make his magic powerful.

After much wandering he stumbled upon Belvedere Castle. Gargamel smashed open the lock on the basement door and stepped inside. "Oh, baby . . . Daddy's home," he said eagerly.

In an apartment across town, a couple was getting the shock of their lives. Patrick Winslow opened the box he had brought home to find five little blue creatures staring up at him!

"Ahhh!" Patrick cried.

In the bathroom Grace Winslow was experiencing a similar shock, having just discovered Clumsy climbing out of the toilet. "Ahhh!" she screamed.

"Please don't hurt me!" Clumsy begged. "I just want to go home."

Grace froze. "Did you just talk?" she asked.

In the living room the other Smurfs were desperately trying to get away from Elway, the dog, and Patrick, who was swatting at them with an umbrella.

"Grace, run!" Patrick shouted. "We're being attacked by tiny . . . talking . . . I don't know whats!"

"It's okay," Grace said gently, coming out of the bathroom with Clumsy in her palm. "They're friendly!"

After everyone had calmed down, the Smurfs told Patrick and Grace all about themselves.

"So you come from a magical forest where you live in oversize mushrooms, you're being chased by an evil wizard and are trapped in New York until there's a blue moon, and you like to say 'smurf' a lot," Patrick said. He still could not believe he was talking to little blue creatures.

"Smurfxactly," Brainy agreed.

"If we're to open the hole to get back home, I'll have to smurf us a
potion to invoke the blue moon," Papa told the Winslows, "but the stars will
need to be perfectly aligned."

Now all Papa needed was a stargazer—but where in this strange land
were they going to find one?

Luckily, Gutsy spotted an ad for a telescope at a toy store. "Stargazer!" he exclaimed. The Smurfs immediately hurried off to find it.

"Focus, everyone," Papa Smurf said as the Smurfs stood with their mouths open inside the huge store. "There's no going home without the stargazer. So spread out and start looking!"

The Smurfs scattered throughout the store, and it wasn't long before kids and their parents noticed them, thinking they were new toys. "It looks like a fat blue ninja!" one kid called out.

"I want one!" cried a little girl.

The crowd was chanting for little blue dolls when Gargamel, who was hot on the Smurfs' trail, entered the store in a rage. Holding up a leaf vacuum, he roared, "Let's pillage this village!"

The Smurfs ran, but Gargamel sucked two of them up with his vacuum: first Brainy and then Gutsy. Papa zoomed by on a skateboard and managed to scoop Smurfette out of the way. Azrael got sucked up instead!

Just then Patrick arrived. He reversed the switch on Gargamel's machine, and Azrael came shooting out, followed by Brainy and Gutsy. As the wizard struggled with the leaf vacuum, the Smurfs and Patrick made their escape. Papa made sure he grabbed a stargazer before he left.

The next morning Papa had good news. "The stars have told me when to smurf the blue moon—we're going home! But it has to be done tonight," he added, "between first star and high moon. That's our only chance. Now we just need the potion that works in this realm."

Following Patrick's advice, the Smurfs found a book in a special bookstore that would help them with the potion and the spell. Papa quickly copied the instructions.

"And these will smurf us a blue moon?" Brainy asked.

"And open the portal," Papa proudly replied.

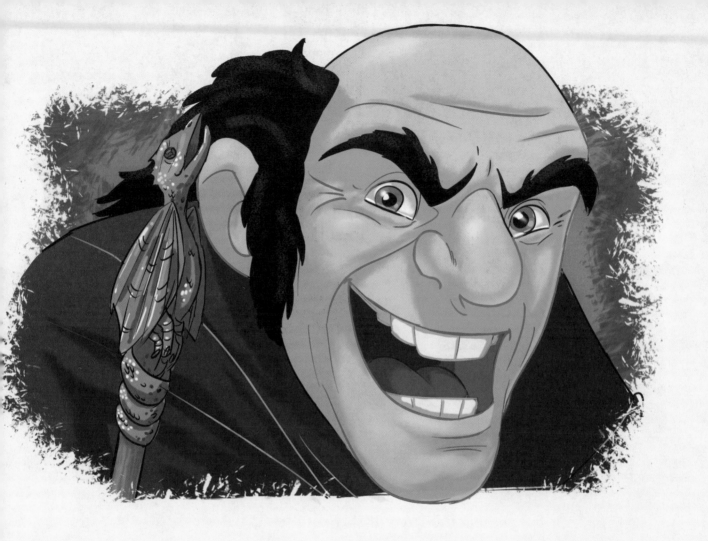

Just as the Smurfs were about to leave the store, Gargamel caught up with them—again!

"Run, Smurfs!" Papa yelled, ordering them to scatter.

Gargamel raised his wand, and a bolt of blue energy zapped toward the Smurfs. Papa grabbed a mirror and blocked the bolt. It hit a large bookcase instead, and Gargamel was suddenly showered with books and dust.

Quickly, Gutsy pulled the grate off a pipe and ushered the Smurfs
through a drain and out of the store. Papa handed the spell to Brainy.

"Smurf the moon tonight," Papa told him.

Brainy was shocked. "Me? Smurf the moon? I'm not ready!"

But Papa looked at him. "You're ready, I know you are. Get everyone
home, Gutsy," Papa continued. "And no matter what happens, don't come
back for me. You'll take care of one another. It's what families do." Then
he went to stall Gargamel, who was fast approaching. With tears in their
eyes, the Smurfs scrambled down the pipe.

Back at the Winslows' apartment, the Smurfs told Patrick and Grace what had happened.

"We promised Papa we wouldn't go back for him!" the Smurfs explained.

"*I* never promised him that," Patrick replied, rushing for the door.

Grace and the Smurfs cheered. "No Smurf left behind!" they cried, following him.

Everyone knew that Gargamel had taken Papa back to Belvedere Castle to extract his Smurf essence. So off they went!

While Patrick, Gutsy, Clumsy, Smurfette, and Grouchy kept watch outside the castle, Brainy was not too far away, mixing up the blue-moon potion. Then he began to recite the spell: "*Soyez calme, le Schtroumpf, etre creer une nouvelle bleue lune . . .*"

POOF! Blue smoke suddenly erupted from the potion and shot into the sky. As the smoke rose and touched the moon, the moon actually turned blue!

Then a swirling portal opened in the nearby waterfall. "I did it!" Brainy cried. He looked over at Belvedere Castle one last time before diving into the hole back to Smurf Village. Brainy's mission was to go back and recruit Smurfs to come back through the portal and help defeat Gargamel.

In the castle Gargamel had Papa strapped into a machine. Suddenly, Grouchy's voice was heard. Papa froze at the sound.

"Did you really think they would go home without you?" Gargamel scoffed. "You're one big happy family!"

Gargamel opened the door to find Grouchy and Clumsy on the terrace walls. They were soon joined by Brainy, who sent a signal for Grace to release dozens of large balloons carrying a heavy bowling ball into the air. When Gutsy saw the balloons, he took off on a remote-controlled flying toy and grabbed them.

Coming face to face with three little Smurfs, Gargamel was amused. "So the *three* of you are going to just . . . bravely gaze down at me until I surrender?" he asked.

"You really should learn to count," Grouchy told the wizard as Brainy lit up the sky with some fireworks. Gargamel suddenly saw that the walls of the castle were covered with Smurfs—and more were coming up behind them! Gargamel raised his wand, but the Smurfs started pelting him with walnuts, eggs, and even a frying pan! Gargamel dropped his wand.

But just as Gutsy let go of the bowling ball above him, Gargamel grabbed it again and shouted, *"Alaca-ZAM!"* A powerful blast of blue energy blew the ball to bits. Raising his wand Gargamel declared, "Behold the awesome power of me!"

Suddenly the wind started to pick up, howling and whirling into a powerful storm. The Smurfs tried hard to hang on, but the wind was too strong and many of them were sucked in. Gargamel then easily snatched each Smurf, and he threw them into his burlap sack.

Meanwhile, Smurfette had found Papa—but first she had to face off with Azrael. Crouching down, Smurfette grabbed the cat's neck and sent him skittering into a stack of cages. One of the cages fell on Azrael, trapping him inside.

"You smurfed with the wrong Smurf," she told the cat before rushing to Papa.

"My little Smurfette!" Papa said proudly, with tears in his eyes. "Where the smurf did you learn to fight like that?"

"What did you expect?" Smurfette replied. "You raised me with ninety-eight brothers!"

Now free, Papa charged at Gargamel in anger, but Gargamel simply turned around and zapped Papa, freezing him in midair.

"Watch closely, Smurfs . . . as Papa meets his little blue end!" Gargamel teased, tossing Papa into the air.

Gargamel flicked his wand and a blast shot out. Patrick charged up the terrace, dove into the air, and caught Papa just in time! The two landed safely behind a low stone wall. The wizard was about to fire another blast when Gutsy appeared on the drone toy and snatched Gargamel's wand!

The Smurfs cheered—and then gasped as Gutsy dropped the wand!
Gargamel let go of his sack in his rush to grab the wand, setting the Smurfs
free. Clumsy raced along the wall to try to catch the wand. "I got it!" he
called, leaping with an outstretched arm. To everyone's surprise, Clumsy
snatched it firmly in his hand!

"Give me my wand!" Gargamel demanded angrily.

But Clumsy pointed the wand at Gargamel—and a strong bolt of energy
shot out, hitting the wizard and pushing him way over the trees.

The Smurfs rushed to lift Clumsy onto their shoulders. "Clum-sy! Clum-sy!
Clum-sy!" they chanted.

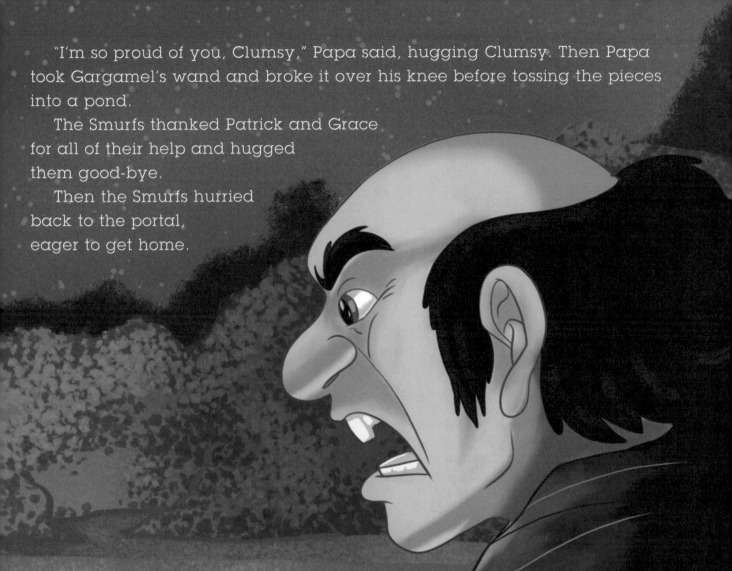

"I'm so proud of you, Clumsy," Papa said, hugging Clumsy. Then Papa took Gargamel's wand and broke it over his knee before tossing the pieces into a pond.

The Smurfs thanked Patrick and Grace for all of their help and hugged them good-bye.

Then the Smurfs hurried back to the portal, eager to get home.

Back in Smurf Village, everyone celebrated at the Blue Moon Festival, the smurfiest night of the year!

"It's smurfin' good to be a Smurf!" Papa exclaimed, happy to be home after such an exciting adventure in the big city!